SUPERMAN™

TALES OF THE FORTRESS OF SOLITUDE

RAYS OF DOOM

by
MICHAEL DAHL

illustrated by
LUCIANO VECCHIO
& TIM LEVINS

Superman created by
JERRY SIEGEL AND JOE SHUSTER
BY SPECIAL ARRANGEMENT WITH
THE JERRY SIEGEL FAMILY

STONE ARCH BOOKS
a capstone imprint

Published by Stone Arch Books
A Capstone Imprint
1710 Roe Crest Drive
North Mankato, Minnesota 56003
www.mycapstone.com

STAR37443

Cataloging-in-Publication Data is available on the Library of Congress website.

ISBN: 978-1-4965-4396-7 (library binding)
ISBN: 978-1-4965-4400-1 (paperback)
ISBN: 978-1-4965-4412-4 (eBook PDF)

Summary: When Superman uncovers a meteor of Red Kryptonite, the Man of Steel transforms into half-man, half-ant, complete with antennas! *Daily Planet* photographer Jimmy Olsen must find a way to stop the super hero before the whole city is exterminated!

Designer: Hilary Wacholz

Printed and bound in the United States of America.
010061S17

TABLE OF CONTENTS

THE FORTRESS OF SOLITUDE

Behold the secret headquarters of Superman.

The Fortress of Solitude contains a lab, a museum, a zoo of alien creatures, and thousands of trophies from the Man of Steel's adventures.

In one corner, Superman safely keeps a hunk of Red Kryptonite in a protective case. Here's the tale behind that souvenir . . .

DAILY
LANET

CHAPTER 1

BUGGING OUT

"This really bugs me!" says Jimmy Olsen. He is a photographer for the *Daily Planet* newspaper.

"What's wrong?" asks Clark Kent, Jimmy's coworker.

"Why do we have to do a story about insects flying through the city?" says Jimmy. "That's not big news."

“Those bugs look pretty big to me,” Clark says.

A swarm of giant ants flies toward the city of Metropolis.

Jimmy snaps photos as the ants fly closer.

“You’re right, Clark!” says Jimmy. “Those babies are huge!”

The swarm streams into the streets of the city.

Suddenly, the ants swoop down in an angry attack.

Men and women scream and run for shelter.

Clark Kent, who is secretly Superman, darts away while no one is looking.

Jimmy keeps snapping pictures during the attack.

A red and blue blur flashes into view.

"Superman!" cries Jimmy.

The Man of Steel shoots skyward like a rocket.

"I must stop these creatures from harming the good people of Metropolis," says Superman.

"Good luck!" Jimmy shouts.

The boy is worried.

Superman is outnumbered by the insect enemy a million to one.

SEEING RED

High above the city, Superman is surrounded by the angry swarm.

"Now that I've got your attention," says the Man of Steel, "let's get down to business."

SWOOSH! The hero plunges downward and smashes through the ground.

Superman tunnels faster and faster.

The ants follow closely behind.

I don't know where they came from, thinks the hero. *But maybe I can find them a new underground home.*

Superman crashes through layers of rock.

Soon, he bursts into a hidden cavern.

"It's the perfect place," says Superman.

Then he freezes.

At the bottom of the cavern glows a hunk of strange crystals.

It is Red Kryptonite!

MUTANT

Red Kryptonite comes from Superman's home planet of Krypton.

The rays of Red Kryptonite have always had a weird effect on the Man of Steel.

What will it do to me this time? wonders Superman. He doesn't have long to wait.

His right arm tingles and begins changing shape. The hero's legs stretch out and bend backward.

An antenna sprouts from his head!

Above ground, the people of Metropolis hear a loud hum.

The swarm of ants has returned.

The flying creatures pour out of the ground and into the air.

At the head of the swarm flies their new leader.

Superman is now a dangerous bug-man!

The mutant super hero can no longer understand humans. He can only communicate with his swarm of followers.

He only knows that his bug friends need a new home.

They need food.

Metropolis will give them both.

But the humans will have to go!

CHAPTER 4

DEADLY RAYS

As soon as Jimmy Olsen sees the mutant Superman, he rushes off to S.T.A.R. Labs.

He hopes that the scientists there can help him save Metropolis.

And save his friend.

“Sounds like Red Kryptonite,” says Professor Potter.

“Red?” says Jimmy. “I thought Kryptonite was green.”

"When Superman's home planet, Krypton, exploded years ago," says the professor, "small chunks of the planet flew off into space."

"There is Green, Red, and even Gold Kryptonite," he adds. "Green Kryptonite can weaken and perhaps kill Superman. Red Kryptonite always does strange things to him."

"Will Superman be a giant ant forever?" asks Jimmy.

"No," says Professor Potter. "The effects only last for several hours."

"Those bugs could destroy the whole city in a few hours!" says Jimmy. "You have to help me stop them!"

A little later, Jimmy rushes back to Metropolis.

He is flying in one of the *Daily Planet* helicopters.

"Superman!" comes the boy's voice from the helicopter's speaker.

"Superman, this is your old friend Jimmy Olsen."

DAILY PLANET

The mutant Superman cannot understand the human words buzzing through the air.

Instead, he decides the strange flying machine is an enemy.

Superman uses his antennas to command his army of ants.

SWOOSH!

The hero chases after the copter.

The angry ants swiftly follow their leader.

Jimmy's hands are sweaty on the copter's controls. *I hope the professor's plan works,* he thinks.

Jimmy pushes a button. A thick green cloud shoots out from the helicopter.

CHAPTER 5

BUG SPRAY

Superman and the ant swarm fly through the cloud as they chase the helicopter.

Soon, the copter shakes under the attack of the powerful bugs.

Jimmy hits the button again and again. More green smoke billows from the copter's jets.

Suddenly, the swarm stops.

Superman's antennas disappear.

His arms and legs shift back to their original shape.

Superman feels weak.

He topples to the ground and lands on the street.

THUD!

The ants are puzzled and confused.

The swarm has lost communication with their new leader.

They fly down and land around Superman, waiting for their next orders.

The Man of Steel lies on the street, not moving.

Slowly, he opens his eyes.

Jimmy Olsen watches from above in his helicopter.

He watches as the Man of Steel slowly stands up.

Then he sees the super hero flash up into the sky.

The ant swarm follows him.

"Sorry about the cloud of Green Kryptonite gas," shouts Jimmy. "Professor Potter thought it would slow you down."

"You saved the day, Jimmy," says Superman.

Superman heads high over the harbor of Metropolis. The ant swarm quickly follows.

After several hours, Superman finds what he is looking for. He locates a deserted island in the Pacific Ocean.

In the middle of the island is a volcano.

Superman's X-ray vision sees through the rock of the volcano. Inside are hundreds of tunnels.

He also sees a cave filled with ant eggs.

Superman figures this is where the ants came from.

A tropical storm must have blown the swarm off course.

As soon as Superman lands on the top of the volcano, the ants all know what to do.

They each return to their different tasks, with many of them looking after the precious eggs.

"Man or insect," says Superman. "There's no place like home."

The next day, Superman is disguised once more as reporter Clark Kent.

Jimmy Olsen's photo is on the cover of the newspaper.

"What do you think?" Jimmy asks. "Pretty cool, huh?"

"It's more than just cool," Clark replies. "I'd say it's *swarm*!"

DAILY PLANET
DAILY PLANET
BUZZ OFF!

GLOSSARY

antenna (an-TEN-uh)—a feeler on the head of an insect

communicate (kuh-MYOO-nuh-kate)—to share information, ideas, or feelings with another by talking, writing, or other means

deserted (di-ZUR-tid)—abandoned and completely empty

disguised (diss-GIZED)—dressed in a way that hides someone's true identity

Kryptonite (KRYP-tuh-nite)—radioactive rocks from the planet Krypton; different colored Kryptonite can weaken or affect Superman.

Krypton (KRYP-tohn)—Superman's home planet

mutant (MYOOT-uhnt)—a living thing that has developed characteristics that are different than the norm

swarm (SWORM)—a group of insects that gather and move in large numbers

DISCUSS

1. Do you believe Jimmy Olsen knows that Clark Kent is really Superman? Why or why not? Use examples from the story to support your answer.

2. Who is the greater hero of this story: Superman or Jimmy Olsen? Explain.

3. If you could transform into any insect, what bug would you be and why?

WRITE

1. Write your own tale of Superman! What villain will the hero face next? Who will he save? The choice is up to you!

2. Create your own color of Kryptonite. Then write a paragraph about how your Kryptonite affects the Man of Steel.

3. In this story, Jimmy Olsen helps his friend Superman. Write your own story about a time that you helped a friend in need.

AUTHOR

Michael Dahl is the author of more than 200 titles for young adults and children, including *The Last Son of Krypton*. He once saw and touched the very first Superman comic book. He is now convinced that he came from another planet and was adopted by his current parents, but they aren't talking.

ILLUSTRATORS

Luciano Vecchio was born in 1982 and is based in Buenos Aires, Argentina. He has illustrated many DC Super Heroes books for Capstone, and his recent comic work includes Beware the Batman, Green Lantern: The Animated Series, Young Justice, Ultimate Spider-Man, and his creator-owned webcomic, *Sereno*.

Tim Levins is best known for his work on the Eisner Award-winning DC Comics series Batman: Gotham Adventures. Tim has illustrated other DC titles, such as Justice League Adventures, Batgirl, Metal Men, and Scooby-Doo, and has also done work for Marvel Comics and Archie Comics. Tim enjoys life in Midland, Ontario, Canada, with his wife, son, dog, and two horses.